SESAME STREET

Featuring Jim Henson's
Sesame Street Muppets

A Sesame Street Christmas

by PAT TORNBORG
illustrated by TOM COOKE

A SESAME STREET/GOLDEN PRESS BOOK
Published by Western Publishing Company, Inc.
in conjunction with Children's Television Workshop.

CONTENTS

CHRISTMAS was just a week away and it was raining when Oscar the Grouch splashed into the park. He found all his friends from Sesame Street gathered under Big Bird's umbrella.

"Why all the long faces?" asked Oscar.

"We can't have any Christmas fun without snow," said Prairie Dawn.

"I can't build my Bert snowman," said Ernie.

"I can't count the snowflakes," said the Count.

"Me no eat snow-cones," said Cookie Monster.

Everyone nodded and looked miserable.

"This is just great," said Oscar. "Nobody has any of that Christmas spirit they're always nagging *me* about! It's going to be a damp and gloomy holiday after all. Whoopee!"

"Not so fast, Oscar! We're not giving up on Christmas spirit yet!" said Betty Lou. "Come on, everybody. Let's go to my house for milk and cookies."

Everyone ate six cookies and drank two glasses of milk and felt a little cheerier.

"Who cares about the rain?" said Bert.

"Let's have a terrific Christmas Eve party, anyway!" said Ernie.

"We can sing Christmas carols and tell stories at the party," said Big Bird, brightening.

"Sure," said Betty Lou. "I can read you a Christmas poem right now. My grandfather reads it to me every Christmas. It's about the time there was too much snow for Christmas. Listen."

THE NIGHT BEFORE CHRISTMAS
ON SESAME STREET

T'was the night before Christmas on Sesame Street,
And a stormy one, too, with the snow and the sleet!
All the kids in the neighborhood, snug in pajamas,
Were saying good-night to their papas and mamas.

The house was all quiet at Ernie and Bert's
As they climbed into bed in their cozy nightshirts.
And even outside, everyone was at rest—
The Grouch in his can and the Bird in his nest.

There was one little house where not all was so comfy—
T'was the home of that famous magician named Mumfy.
He feared that the blizzard would keep Santa away,
And he thought of a bleak Christmas morn with dismay.

"This storm might be too much for Santa," he said,
"So I'll conjure some toys for the children instead."
 Then he snatched up his wand, and before he could say
"A la Peanut Butter Sandwiches!" he was on his way.

 A little past midnight, Ernie jumped out of bed.
 He'd been jolted awake by a "thump" overhead.
 As he peered at the roof, he said, "Gee, Bert, that's funny.
 I thought Santa had reindeer, but that looks like a bunny!"

 Ernie raced to the living room just as a foot
 Had emerged from the chimney, all covered with soot.
 The body that followed was equally grubby.
 Said Ernie, "Why, *this* Santa's not even chubby!

"His face is all dirty, his cloak's black as night.
 But I always thought Santa wore red and white!
 He has only a stick poking out of his pouch,
 And these gifts should have gone to Oscar the Grouch!"

Ernie hopped back in bed and was soon sound asleep,
But poor Mumford had other appointments to keep.
With his team of white rabbits, the brave little wizard
Continued his trip through the terrible blizzard.

Mumfie's magic did wonders on that Christmas Eve,
But the gifts it created were hard to believe!
There was seed for a bird by the Count's Christmas tree,
And the sneakers for Big Bird were only size three!

Little Grover had hoped for a new teddy bear,
But his gift was a ribbon for Betty Lou's hair.
And if you think that Grover was pretty unlucky,
Bert's soap dish was intended for poor Rubber Duckie.

As the morning came, Mumford drove home through the drifts.
He had made all his rounds, given everyone gifts.
So imagine his shock when he walked in to see
A fat, jolly old man sitting there by his tree!

"Mumford, my friend," Santa said with a smile,
"I've been two steps behind you for quite a long while.
 Though you made some unusual gift selections,
 You've done a fine job, with my little corrections.

"I followed your sleigh and erased all your traces.
 You left all the right gifts, but in all the wrong places!
 I just made a few switches so no one would know
 That old Santa Claus was held up by the snow.

"But the meaning of Christmas is not gifts, my boy;
 It's the impulse to do things that bring others joy.
 Though your magical wand can't do everything right,
 The true magic of Christmas was with you tonight!"

With a nod of his head and a wink of his eye
Santa hopped in his sleigh and took off for the sky.
He was heard to exclaim as he flew out of sight,
"A LA PEANUT BUTTER SANDWICHES!
    AND TO ALL A GOOD NIGHT!"

"Thanks for that poem, Betty Lou," said Big Bird. "Now I'm not worried about the rain or the snow."

"Oh, neither am I," said Grover. "Christmas is Christmas, whatever the weather!"

WET CHRISTMAS

"I think white Christmases are yucchy! My uncle Bing Grouchby sang a hit song years ago that describes exactly what Christmas should be like."

I'm dreaming of a wet Christmas,
Just like the ones I used to know.
When the kids stay inside,
And they can't sleigh-ride,
Because there's rain instead of snow!
    Ho, ho, ho, ho, ho, ho...
I'm calling for a wet Christmas
For every person that I've met.
Yes, it's puddles I'm hoping you'll get,
And may *all* your Christmases be wet!

BIG BIRD'S BIRD FEEDER

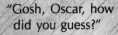

"Gosh, Oscar, how did you guess?"

"We could be out splashing people, and *you* want to stay here and hang peanut butter and seeds on your tree, Big Bird? If you ask me, it's for the birds!"

Here's what you need to make an outdoor tree for your feathered friends:

6 wooden clip clothespins
6 heavy foil cupcake cups
½ cup of birdseed
¼ cup of peanut butter
½ cup of bacon fat or lard
1 cup of cornmeal
glue that won't dissolve in water
a grownup to help you

Here's what you do:

1. Melt the fat in a saucepan, and let it cool for a little while.
2. Add the birdseed, peanut butter, and cornmeal. Stir everything up with a wooden spoon.
3. Spoon some of the mixture into each foil cup.
4. Put the cups of bird cake in the refrigerator until they harden a bit.
5. Remove the cups from the refrigerator and put a blob of glue on the bottom of each cup. Glue each cup onto one flat side of a clothespin. Let the glue dry.
6. Pin the cakes onto the branches of a tree, and watch the birds enjoy their Christmas dinner!

NUTCRACKER SWEETS

"I cracked nuts all day long to make my favorite Christmas treats for the Christmas Eve party. Ya!"

"Oh, my goodness, Herry. What a lot of nuts you have here. It must have taken a very long time to get them all out of their cute little shells."

Candied Nuts

Here's what you need to make candied nuts:

½ cup brown sugar, packed firm
¼ cup granulated sugar
⅓ cup half-and-half milk and cream
½ teaspoon almond extract
1½ cups whole almonds
a candy thermometer
a grownup to help you

Here's what you do:

Put all the sugar and the half-and-half into a saucepan and stir over low heat until the sugar is dissolved. Continue to cook over low heat, without stirring, until the temperature, measured on a candy thermometer, reaches 240 degrees. The mixture will be syrupy, and will form a soft ball when a little bit is dropped into cold water.

Add the almond extract and the almonds, and stir the nuts until they are coated with the syrup. Spoon them out onto wax paper or foil, and separate them with a fork. As they cool, the coating will harden.

You will have two cups of candied nuts.

"What's a nutcracker?"

"You must be very handy with a nutcracker, Herry."

Spiced Nuts

Here's what you need to make spiced nuts:

1 tablespoon egg white
2 cups pecans or walnuts
⅓ cup sugar
1 tablespoon cinnamon
¼ teaspoon nutmeg

Here's what you do:

Put the nuts into a mixing bowl and add the egg white. Stir until all the nuts are sticky.

Mix the sugar and spices. Sprinkle the mixture on the nuts and stir until the nuts are coated with it. Spread the nuts on an ungreased baking sheet and ask a grownup to bake them in a 300° oven for 30 minutes. Makes two cups of spiced nuts.

"My bottle cap collection always brings back fond memories. This cap is from a Figgy Fizz I drank last Arbor Day in the park. And this cap is from the bottle I used to make some frozen Figgy Pops just last Tuesday. Now I need to use these bottle caps to make Ernie's Christmas present. Oh, well. I still have my oatmeal box collection."

to: ERNIE
from: BERT

Here's what you need to make picture ornaments:

a bunch of bottle caps
some pictures from magazines or old Christmas cards
glue
yarn

Here's what you do:

1. Cut out some beautiful little pictures in circles just big enough to fit inside a bottle cap.
2. Glue the pictures inside the bottle caps with a dab of glue.
3. Put another dab of glue on the back of the bottle cap and stick on a long piece of yarn.

4. Tie the yarn in a loop with a pretty bow.
5. Hang these cute little framed pictures on your Christmas tree.
   After Christmas, you can hang them in your room—from a
   bedpost, a doorknob, a picture hook, or anywhere!

"This pile of old oatmeal boxes gives me a great idea for Bert's Christmas present. I know he'd love a set of rhythm drums, and just think how happy he'll be that I found something to do with these old boxes! He won't even miss them. He still has his bottle cap collection."

Here's what you need to make rhythm drums:

one round oatmeal box for each drum
several sheets of construction paper in different colors
paste
gold or silver stick-on stars
colored cord or yarn

Here's what you do:

1. Take the lids off the boxes and cut each box straight around to the height you want it.
2. Cut a piece of colored paper to fit around the whole box.
3. Cover the box with paste and smooth on the paper.
4. Trace around the box lid on different colored paper to make two circles.

5. Cut out the paper circles and paste them on the lid and the bottom of the oatmeal box.

6. From a third color of paper, cut two strips to fit around the rims of the lid and the base of the box.

7. Put the lid back on the box and paste the strips around the top and bottom of the box.

8. Stick the cord or yarn on with the stick-on stars. Drums of different heights make different sounds. The more drums you make, the better the music will be!

PASTE

A CHRISTMAS POEM
by Big Bird

Everybody seems to think that
Christmas comes just once a year,
On December twenty-fifth. Or so they say.
But I remember other times
That were really very special,
And I know they didn't come on Christmas Day!

In the spring I had the sniffles
And was feeling simply awful,
And I didn't know exactly what to do.
Mr. Hooper brought me chicken soup,
And soon I was all better.
And you know, that really seemed
    like Christmas, too!

At our street bazaar last summer
Betty Lou won all the pies.
Now, I must admit, that seemed a bit unfair.
But when she cut them into pieces,
And she gave us each a slice,
Did you notice there was Christmas in the air?

In the fall, when Herry's kitten
Climbed a tree and she got stuck,
I knew that I would have to do my part.
So I stretched myself real tall
And I gave a helping hand,
With a Christmas kind of feeling in my heart.

I am sure it doesn't matter
If it rains or if it snows.
Christmas doesn't seem to care about the weather.
Being good to one another
Summer, winter, fall and spring
Makes it Christmastime whenever we're together.

WHITE CHRISTMAS

I dreamed of snow for Christmas.
There were visions in my head
Of a snowball fight, a snowman,
And me riding on my sled.

If there isn't snow for Christmas,
I will simply have to fake it.
If I can't go out and play in it,
I'll just stay home and make it!

Make paper snowflakes to put in your windows or hang on your tree:

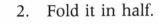

1. Start with a square of paper, any size.

2. Fold it in half.

3. Fold it in half again.

4. Fold it diagonally to make a triangle.

5. Cut small shapes out of all sides. Unfold.

Dessert Snowballs
(makes 4)

Here's what you need:

1 pint vanilla ice cream
½ cup shredded coconut
ice cream scoop

Here's what you do:

Spread the coconut out on a large plate. Scoop out four round balls of ice cream. Using two spoons, gently roll the ice cream balls in the coconut. When they're completely coated with coconut, put them in the freezer until you're ready to eat them.

THE COUNT'S TWELVE DAYS OF CHRISTMAS CALENDAR

Do you know the song,
The Twelve Days of Christmas?
This is The Count's own version.

On the *first* day of
Christmas
My good friends gave
to me

One new bat for my
belfry.

On the *second* day of
Christmas
My good friends gave
to me

Two spiffy spats.

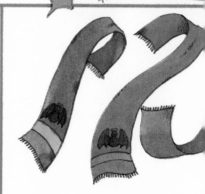

On the *third* day of
Christmas
My good friends gave
to me

Three silk scarves.

On the *seventh* day of
Christmas
My good friends gave
to me

Seven jersey jackets.

On the *eighth* day of
Christmas
My good friends gave
to me

Eight nifty neckties.

On the *ninth* day of
Christmas
My good friends gave
to me

Nine silly sashes.

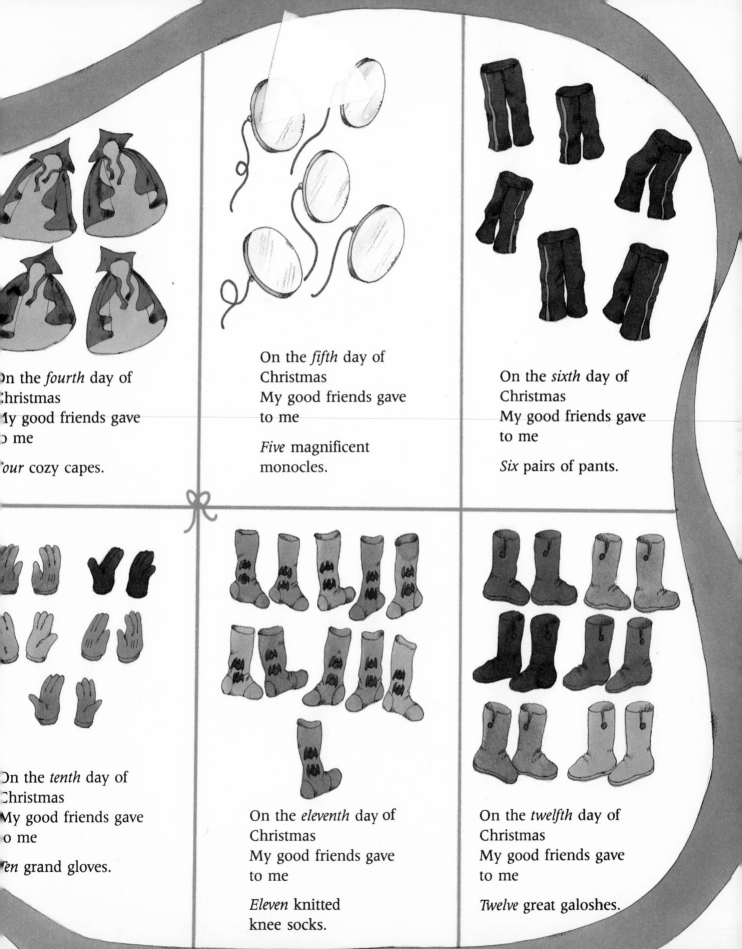

On the *fourth* day of Christmas
My good friends gave to me

Four cozy capes.

On the *fifth* day of Christmas
My good friends gave to me

Five magnificent monocles.

On the *sixth* day of Christmas
My good friends gave to me

Six pairs of pants.

On the *tenth* day of Christmas
My good friends gave to me

Ten grand gloves.

On the *eleventh* day of Christmas
My good friends gave to me

Eleven knitted knee socks.

On the *twelfth* day of Christmas
My good friends gave to me

Twelve great galoshes.

OSCAR'S CHRISTMAS CAROL
(A Dickens of a Story)

"BAH, HUMBUG!" Oscar said loudly just as Big Bird and Betty Lou walked by. "Bah, humbug!" he said again as they stopped to stare.

"Whatever that means, it sure sounds grouchy," said Betty Lou. "What's the matter, Oscar?"

"Nothing's the matter," Oscar answered. "Everything's great. I'm reading a terrific story about a mean old fellow named Mr. Scrooge. He hated Christmas, so he said, 'Bah, humbug!' all the time. He sounds just like my uncle Smarmy. He might even be a relative of mine!"

"How could anyone hate Christmas?" asked Betty Lou. "Everyone is good and kind at Christmas, and there are good things to eat, and songs to sing and presents to give. Christmas is a happy time, Oscar."

"Bah, humbug!" Oscar replied. "Mr. Scrooge had a way of fixing that. Not only was he miserable himself, but he ruined everyone else's Christmas, too. He even made his helper, Bob Cratchit, work on Christmas Eve! Boy, that's a real grouch for you!"

"Hey, wait a minute," said Big Bird. "I know that story. It's 'A Christmas Carol,' by Mr. Charles Dickens. Maria read it to me last Christmas. And guess what, Oscar. It has a happy ending!"

"How could it?" asked Oscar in disgust. "This guy Scrooge was such a great grouch! He's my hero—an inspiration! I want to be just like him."

"Well, then," said Big Bird, "you'll have to stop being a grouch, because that's what Scrooge did. He had a dream that showed him how wrong he had been about Christmas. You should read the rest of the book, Oscar."

"Bah, humbug," said Oscar as he disappeared into his can.

A little later, Big Bird passed Oscar's can again on his way home from Betty Lou's house. "Merry Christmas, Bird!" shouted Oscar as he popped out.

Big Bird looked at Oscar in surprise. "Why, Oscar, you changed your mind. You must have had a dream, just like Mr. Scrooge did, and now you're not going to be a grouch any more!"

"Ho, ho, ho, no, no, no!" said Oscar. "That's not what happened. I was giving that dumb book with the happy ending to the trash man just after you left, and he reminded me that Christmas is a *holiday.* You know what that means, Bird?"

"Sure," said Big Bird. "A holiday is a day when everyone is good and kind and celebrates..."

"No, no," broke in Oscar. "It means that there's no trash pick-up that day, and I get to keep my wonderful trash one more day! What a gift! Merry Christmas, Bird!"

COOKIE MONSTER'S CHRISTMAS TREE

"Me in big trouble, Betty Lou! Me want to hang pretty cookies on tree, but cookies always look good enough to eat."

"I'll help you make some cookies that even *you* won't eat, Cookie Monster. Then you can put them on your tree instead."

Here's what you need to make "cookie" ornaments:

1 can of children's white or yellow air-drying modelling compound
ribbon or yarn
a pencil
watercolor paints
bread board and small rolling pin
clear shellac

Here's what you do:

1. Roll out a chunk of the modelling dough with the rolling pin until it is about ⅛ of an inch thick.
2. Cut out cookie shapes, using either cookie cutters or a drinking glass.
3. Punch a hole with the pencil about ¼ inch from the top of the "cookie" shape.
4. Let the "cookies" dry overnight and then decorate them with watercolor paints.
5. After the paint has dried, cover the "cookies" with shellac if you want them to last.
6. Thread the ribbon or yarn through the holes, tie some nice bows, and hang these "cookie" ornaments on your tree.

Note: To make your own modeling dough, take one slice of stale white bread without crusts and one-half teaspoon of white glue for each "cookie." Knead chunks of bread with glue until the mixture feels like dough. Children can shape and flatten "cookies" with their hands. Then follow steps 3 to 6.

THE COUNT'S CHRISTMAS TREE

"Cutouts of my darling bats in their little holiday outfits make wonderful decorations. Would you like to make some for your Christmas tree? Don't forget to hang them upside down. Bats will be bats!"

Here's how to make batty ornaments:

1. Trace these batty ornaments and paste the tracings onto light cardboard.
2. Color and decorate the bats. Then cut them out.
3. Ask a grownup to poke holes for yarn loops.
4. Hang them on a Christmas tree or a mantle, or in the window.

Here's how to make foil chains:

1. Cut or tear aluminum foil into pieces about six inches long and about half as wide.
2. Crush or roll the pieces into strips and crinkle the ends together to form a "link."
3. Slip the next rolled-up foil strip through the first link before crinkling the ends together.
4. Make as many as you need to reach around your Christmas tree. The Count counts his links as he works.

"Here's how I make shiny chains to hang on my tree. It's easy to do, and they look just like the real chains hanging around my castle."

JOLLY OLD SAINT NICHOLAS

Jolly old Saint Nicholas,
Lean your ear this way.
Don't you tell a single soul
What I'm going to say.
Christmas Eve is coming soon.
Now, you dear old man,
Whisper what you'll bring to me.
Tell me if you can.

When the clock is striking twelve,
When we're fast asleep,
Down the chimney broad and black
With your pack you'll creep.
All the stockings you will find,
Hanging in neat rows.
Mine's the one you'll notice first,
'Cause it has three toes!

Ernie wants a little friend
For his Rubber Duckie.
Oscar wants a worn-out shoe.
He thinks toys are yucchy!
Bert would like some bottle caps,
But for me, Saint Nick,
I'd prefer to be surprised,
So I'll let *you* pick!

THOUGHTS
THAT COUNT

Dear Mommy,
How can I help you?
Let me count the ways!
I can keep my bedroom tidy,
And be good on rainy days.
I am sure to be a little help
In everything you do.
Why, there must be a million ways
To show that I love you!

Here is a way to give your best gift—yourself!
Give gift cards that make promises you can keep!

Dear Batty,
I promise not to wake
you up in the morning.

Let me
take the
trash
out for
you.

THE COUNT'S CHRISTMAS CASTLE

One wonderful drawbridge
Leads to *two* marvelous doors.
There are *three* adorable windows,
And the towers come in *fours*.
Add *five* licorice candies,
And *six* black jelly drops.
Make *seven* peppermint bushes.
The *eight* trees are lollipops.
The snow is made from icing;
You can put on any amount.
Everything you put on your castle,
You must surely remember to *count!*

Here's what you need to make a wonderful castle just like mine:

*1 cardboard box, about 12 inches long,
   10 inches wide and 7 inches deep*
*1 flat piece of cardboard for the "lawn,"
   about 15 inches by 20 inches*
colorful string
white glue
tape
4 toothpicks
a small piece of wrapping paper
2 one-pound boxes of graham crackers
1 one-pound box of confectioner's sugar
4 ice cream cones
whites of 3 eggs

You will need assorted candies for details:

*1 chocolate bar that can be broken
   in square sections (for windows)*
5 licorice pieces
6 black jelly drops
7 peppermints
8 lollipops
red cherry whips (for outlining)
*assorted colorful hard candies
   (for outlining)*

This amount of candy will cover the front of the castle. You will need additional candy to decorate all four sides.

Here's what you do:

1. Lay the box on one of its twelve-inch sides on the flat cardboard "lawn" and cut into the bottom flap as shown, so you have an open doorway and a drawbridge the width of two graham crackers.

2. Glue graham crackers on the whole box and the drawbridge.

3. Fill in all the cracks on the box walls with icing "cement."

4. Attach other pieces with the icing as the picture shows: 2 crackers for doors, sections of chocolate bar for each window, ice cream cones for towers, and so on.

5. Spread any leftover icing onto the flat cardboard for snow, and plant lollipop trees.

6. Cut 4 waving banners out of wrapping paper and glue them onto 4 toothpicks. Poke the toothpicks carefully through the points of the cone towers. Glue string from door to drawbridge.

To make the icing:

1. Beat the three egg whites with an eggbeater until they just start to get fluffy.

2. Little by little, stir in 3 cups of confectioners' sugar with a wooden spoon. The final mixture should be quite stiff and pasty. (The more sugar you add, the faster and harder the icing will dry.)

A WRAP SESSION

EARLY on Christmas Eve, everyone gathered to wrap presents before the big Christmas party. But nobody had remembered to bring any wrapping paper or ribbons! Just then, Oscar the Grouch arrived with his gifts all wrapped up in newspaper and tied with bits of old string.

"Hey, Oscar, what a good idea!" said Betty Lou. "We don't need fancy paper and ribbons. We can wrap our presents with all kinds of things we find around the house!"

Just as they were finishing wrapping the gifts, Prairie Dawn
looked out the window. "Oh, look!" she cried. "It's snowing! It's
going to be a white Christmas after all! Let's go caroling."
And that's just what they did.

WE WISH YOU A MERRY CHRISTMAS

We wish you a merry Christmas
We wish you a merry Christmas
We wish you a merry Christmas
And a happy New Year!

We all want some Figgy Fizz punch
We all want some Figgy Fizz punch
We all want some Figgy Fizz punch
So bring it right here!

We won't go until we get some
We won't go until we get some
We won't go until we get some
It's a cup of good cheer!

BERT'S RECIPES

Bert's Aunt Willy's Crispy Oatmeal Cookies

1 stick butter
⅓ cup of sugar
2¼ cups of oats

Let the butter soften at room temperature so you can work it with your hands. Put all the ingredients into a mixing bowl and knead them until they're well blended. Roll the dough into walnut-size balls. On a board, flatten the balls with the back of a fork until they are very thin. Use a spatula to transfer the cookies to an ungreased baking sheet. Ask a grownup to bake them for about eight minutes, or until golden brown, in a 325° oven.

Bert's Figgy Fizz Punch
(Serves 4)

One 11-ounce jar of whole figs in syrup, chilled
Two 10-ounce cans of root beer

Put a whole fig and one tablespoon of syrup into four glasses. Fill up each glass with root beer and stir. Serve Figgy Fizz Punch with long spoons so everyone can eat the fig in the bottom of each glass.